"The End of Superman"

And Other Short Stories

By

David B. Tick

ISBN: 0-7596-6281-9 (e-book)
ISBN: 0-7596-6282-7 (Paperback)

This book is printed on acid free paper.

1stBooks - rev. 07/30/04

Illustrations
by Christopher Crocker

This book is dedicated to

the teachers of contemporary literature.

Table of Contents

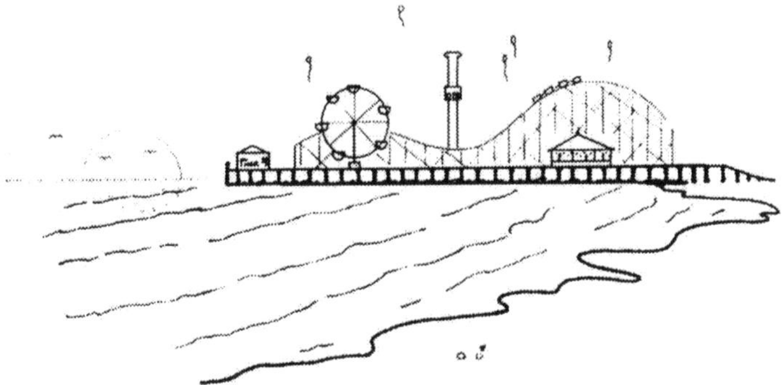

"New England Home Grown"

Special Thanks!
Joe Amico
Alan Belinfante
John Cecca Jr.
Joe Ciampa
Debbie Hartman
Karen Malfitano
Tom Misci
Paul Rizzo
Joe Siciliano

OCEAN CITY

I grew up in the quaint, little town of Port James, which is shaped almost like a horseshoe and situated on the New England coast. When I was a very young boy, probably about five or six years old, my parents began to take me to Ocean City, especially during the summers. Ocean City had a very popular amusement park that featured a classic wooden roller coaster and a Ferris wheel as well as all of the standard rides. The aroma of popcorn and hot dogs would mix with the fresh, salty air to create a perfect atmosphere for almost any afternoon or evening.

Fancy sports cars and outrageous looking motorcycles roared up and down the boulevard between the amusement park and the beach... as families would sit on the sea wall to have something to eat, or just kick back and relax. At dusk, the outline of clam diggers on the shoreline was a familiar sight during low tide.

Sometimes my parents would take me swimming there for the entire day. Ocean City had a beautiful, sandy beach with spectacular island views over the horizon. Although Port James bordered Ocean City, the beaches at Port James were rocky and mostly located in the bay, which meant that we didn't have the large waves like the ones so prevalent in Ocean City.

I was an only child. My parents were both history professors who had met while teaching at the same community college. I wouldn't say that my upbringing was particularly restrictive, and that was probably because my parents were always cognizant of what they would refer to as "not crushing my spirit." Basically, as long as I did well in school and stayed out of trouble, I had quite a bit of freedom compared to most of my friends.

Right around the time that I reached my tenth birthday, I met Albie, who was also ten. His real name was Albert, but nobody ever called him that. I think he inherited that name from his great-grandfather but disinherited it on his own. The circumstances of our introduction were more than unusual in that we almost knocked each other unconscious on the bumper cars one late afternoon at the amusement park. We were two young kids who had never seen each other before… just buzzing around, smashing into every car that we could… and ignoring our parents' warnings as well as the posted signs about avoiding head-on collisions! From about thirty feet apart, we lined each other up and then it was *pedal to the metal*. Upon impact, they actually had to turn off the electricity and check to see if we were okay. I remember the attendant and my parents standing over me… as Albie's parents were helping *him* out of the little car. From that moment on, Albie and I became the best of friends. Our parents would also become close, and they would go out together socially, quite often.

For all of the surrounding communities, Ocean City was definitely the most exciting place to visit, and becoming friends with Albie had other advantages besides our great friendship. He lived less than a mile from the amusement park and directly across the street from the best part of the beach where you could dive off the jetties into deep water. As time moved on, I would stay over on the weekends. Since Albie was also an only child, we became like family, and we referred to each other as "cousins." During the summers, we would have some great barbecues at his house. In my mind, I can still see his father standing in their backyard wearing a full-length apron and holding grilling utensils. Albie's family owned an insurance agency in Ocean City. His parents had a great sense of humor unlike my parents who had a more serious nature, which I think was because of their immersion into the campus politics of the day… you know… social justice, the environment, and various "hot" topics like abortion and euthanasia. It was interesting to see how their personalities would change around Albie's parents… always laughing and joking. I wish that they could have been a little more like that when they were at home.

Upon entering middle school, my parents began to let me explore the world outside of our immediate neighborhood, and I was even able to convince them that I was old enough to bicycle the four miles to Albie's house on Saturday mornings a couple of times a month. Sometimes the trip was *less* than a leisurely ride to a friend's house and more like an obstacle course. After the first mile out of Port James bordering Ocean City, there was a large hill with hundreds of trees on the left side of the street; and on any given day, hundreds of crab apples would rain down on unsuspecting travelers, courtesy of some Ocean City kids giving a hearty welcome to their Port James neighbors. If you escaped that onslaught, there were always a few "punks" who might try to take your bike. The way to avoid trouble was to go fairly early in the morning, between eight and nine o'clock. The bike ride to Albie's house would take me about twenty-five minutes… if the wind wasn't blowing against me.

After spending the day there, his parents would put my bike into the trunk of their car and drive me home.

Most of the time they would come in for a visit with my folks and listen to some music, play bridge, and drink an occasional glass of wine. Albie and I would throw around a baseball or shoot some baskets at the park if it wasn't too dark. Sometimes, we would just go to the beach and skip stones on the water. If there was one thing our beaches had… it was rocks… too many!

The winter months pretty much confined me to Port James, but Albie and I would still hang out on Saturday mornings at the candlepin bowling alley, which also had an indoor miniature golf course in the same building. With his good looks and gregarious personality, Albie was extremely popular with the girls. We always had female bowling and golf partners, which helped me to overcome my youthful shyness. As the weather became warmer, we would all go on the rides together, eat pizza, play the arcade games, and then go swimming. Those were great times!

TWO PLUS ONE

During the summer after my freshman year of high school, Albie introduced me to his friend, Jimbo, a very short guy… and built like "The Hulk." To us, he was as strong as the Hulk, too. Jimbo and Albie had met while playing football on the beach with some of the other guys from their high school. Jimbo automatically assumed the role of enforcer in our trio and that was fine with me. Just fooling around, Albie and I would grab him from behind, and Jimbo would laugh as he broke our holds by flexing his muscles, which were ripples of steel. He was constantly working out and practicing martial arts.

As a young boy, Jimbo had moved to Ocean City from Port James after his parents divorced, and he lived with his younger sister, mother and aunt (Debbie) in an apartment complex not too far from Albie's house. Jimbo's father still lived in Port James.

Jimbo had a huge crush on this pretty girl named Flo, who was totally infatuated with Albie as were most of the girls, but Jimbo was persistent enough until she finally responded to his advances. Eventually Flo and Jimbo were bowling and miniature golf partners. They would sit together on the rides as well as take walks on the beach and "make out." What neither one of them knew was that they were connected in another way.

Flo's brother, Rocco, and Jimbo had met years earlier at the amusement park's "Shoot Out The Star" game. That fateful autumn day, Rocco had been at the horse track most of the afternoon, picking up the used programs and reselling them outside of the track for half price. Of course this was illegal, but it also was an activity usually done all the time by the younger kids with only minor consequences if they were unlucky enough to be caught by the police. After making about ten dollars, Rocco had decided to go to the amusement park to get something to eat.

Jimbo's Aunt Debbie and her best friend had taken Jimbo to the Penny Arcade that afternoon, a few months after his mother and father had separated. It was his first time visiting Ocean City Amusement Park, and he couldn't have been more than six or seven. Rocco wandered in, eyed the two girls, and applied some of his very limited charm. He almost convinced them to go for hot dogs at the Joe and Nemo stand, but he actually wanted the girls to leave Jimbo alone at the arcade, while he treated only them. That wasn't going to happen and Debbie and her friend let Rocco know exactly what they thought of him.

As the two girls grabbed Jimbo's hand and quickly exited the Penny Arcade, Rocco suddenly ran ahead of them and stopped at the rifle range arcade game, yelling out in their direction that he was going to shoot out the red star with one shot. Rocco proceeded to grab the 22-caliber rifle; there was a chain attached which kept the rifle from pointing away from the target, but the chain wasn't taut. Rocco tried to aim above the girls' heads, but even though the chain was loose, it was fastened tight enough to keep the rifle at a certain height.

In the confusion of trying to service too many customers, the attendant was unable to keep track of which rifles were loaded. Not having even paid yet, Rocco expected to hear a click when he squeezed the trigger, but instead… a shot rang out. Debbie's friend lay on the ground with a bullet hole through her cheek.

Luckily… she survived, but she was left with a disfiguring scar and had to go through many painful reconstructive surgeries over the next few years. Jimbo would go to the hospital with his Aunt Debbie to visit her during those times. Ironically, this incident served Rocco's reputation, as a "gangster wannabe" quite well, and he didn't spend any time in jail because it was ruled an accident. He even said that Debbie's friend was lucky because she received a large financial settlement from the amusement park.

The rifle range was replaced with a B.B. machine-gun game… and "Shoot Out The Star" became "Shoot Out The Dot."

SUNDAY DINNER

Jimbo used to carry around this fake, black, rubber gun that looked pretty real. We would take turns scaring our friends, but we were too young or naïve to understand that a fake gun could get you into as much trouble as a real gun. We learned that the hard way after Flo invited Jimbo to her house for a Sunday dinner. He didn't want to go alone so Albie and I went along with him. It was weird thinking about having a family style dinner with strangers, but we didn't want to say "no" to Jimbo.

Flo's parents were very friendly and the meal was one course after another. I don't think that I had ever tasted food that good. They lived in a beautiful Victorian house with a huge fireplace. Flo's dad was a contractor, and her mom worked as a waitress at the local diner near the dog track. They had friends in Port James, so we talked a little about yacht clubs, sailboats and other things that I knew very little about… like union jobs and working on the docks. Flo and Jimbo sat together; Albie and I were told to sit next to two of Flo's friends who were also invited, I guess, to be our dates. Albie and I had seen them around the bowling alley, but we never hung out with them. Flo was planning that we could all go on the rides together after the dinner, and that was all right with Albie and me.

As we were finishing dessert, Flo's dad spoke to Jimbo in a half serious tone… something about "taking good care of his daughter" at the amusement park. Without really thinking, Jimbo reached under his shirt, pulled out the toy gun and said, "Don't you worry sir; she's in good hands with me!" Jimbo had a big grin on his face.

Flo's mother began to scream like a banshee, and her father almost knocked the table over as he tried to grab the "gun" from Jimbo who was now becoming fully aware that there was a serious problem. Flo and her girlfriends were swearing at Jimbo, as Albie and I rose to our feet wondering why everybody was getting so upset about a rubber toy gun… then again, it did look real to us the first time we had seen it too.

Albie grabbed the "gun" away from Jimbo, and Flo's father took a swing at Jimbo's arm… screaming at him to get the hell out of there and never come back! As we scurried toward the front door, a figure suddenly appeared in front of us. Flo yelled out, "It's my brother Rocco! You guys had better get out of here!" When Jimbo heard Rocco's name, he looked across the room; and for the first time since "the accident," he was face to face with childhood trauma. He didn't recognize Rocco from so many years ago, but he knew in his heart that it was the same person. There just weren't too many people around named Rocco.

As we left the house in a fast walk, Jimbo burst into laughter, and then he put his head down into cupped hands for a few seconds. I couldn't tell if he was still laughing… or crying. Albie jumped on his back and I tackled him to the ground; then we heard Jimbo say," Can you believe Rocco is Flo's brother?" Albie laughed and replied, "Get rid of that stupid gun." Jimbo gave it to me and I think I still have it… somewhere.

TINY

Jimbo and I had become good friends, but we rarely did anything separate from Albie because he was the connection between us. There *was* this one time, however, that for a week Jimbo and I were on our own as the "dynamic duo" because Albie was sick. I had gone to play miniature golf with a few of my friends from Port James, and one of them had decided that he was on a real golf course and swung the club too hard. We all had done that occasionally but usually at an outdoor course, not indoors. The golf ball went sailing across the building, hit a sign and ended up landing right on a lane, finally bouncing into the gutter near some guys who were bowling. One of them spilled his drink as the ball bounced next to him. We knew there might be trouble because they kept on looking our way, but they left before we did.

When we exited the building, there they were waiting outside for us… older, bigger, and tougher. Suddenly out of nowhere, Jimbo just appeared like the superhero he was, jumping out of a car that had driven up over the low curb onto the sidewalk. Obviously sensing that there was trouble, he walked up to one of them and said, "You know me… gotta problem with my friends?" Then he glared up at each one of them. Their attitudes quickly changed, sounding like elementary school children talking to the principal as they told him about the golf ball incident. Jimbo pulled me aside and suggested that my friends treat everyone for pizza as a gesture of friendship… so they did. After that, we started hanging out and actually became friendly with those guys… bowling against them as a team for almost a year. The legend of "The Hulk" was now a part of Port James folklore.

Later on that day after my friends left, Jimbo and I headed over to Albie's house. We had decided to go visit him to see how he was feeling, but his mother just let us in as far as the kitchen and said that Albie was sleeping; he had the "24 hour" flu. It was getting late, so I called my parents and they offered to pick me up, but Jimbo signaled to me that he could get me a ride home… and I had cab fare if necessary. My parents didn't know Jimbo that well, but since I was calling from Albie's house, they assumed that Albie's parents would probably give me a ride if I needed it.

As we walked on the boulevard along the beach across from the amusement park, Jimbo came up with an idea. "Let's go to the poolroom!"

What?" I asked.

"The pool room… on Broadway," he answered.

"Okay, but why don't we just go swimming in the ocean? What is it… a public pool?"

Jimbo just laughed and said, "You guys from Port James live a very sheltered life, and to think that I was once one of you!"

The place was really dark and smelled like a men's room. It was empty except for a couple of drunks who were sitting at the bar with their heads down. Jimbo and I racked up the balls and began to play. I was feeling uneasy because I didn't think we were supposed to be in there. We were only fifteen… but nobody said anything. This was part of Jimbo's world and probably a little bit of Albie's too. From the back of the room, a booming voice suddenly yelled out, "Jimbo, my man!" The voice then revealed himself in the form of a giant.

"Hi Tiny!" Jimbo said.

"*Hi Tiny.*" The giant said in a mocking tone. "What are you kids doing in here? You want me to get busted again?"

Jimbo rolled his eyes.

"Oh yeah," Tiny said, "you're a tough guy." Tiny was about six foot five... three hundred pounds. "Who's your friend?"

Jimbo introduced me as his good buddy from Port James.

"Port James," Tiny snickered, "yacht clubs, coffee shops, hair salons, and liquor stores. That place makes me sick."

I nodded.

"You like Ocean City?"

Jimbo replied for me, "He's always in Ocean City."

Tiny looked at me. "Do you talk?"

"How'd you get the name Tiny?" I blurted out.

"You figure it out genius. Okay, you kids can stay for an hour, but when the regulars come in, you're gone."

We finished playing pool, and then I followed Jimbo into a side room that was down a short hallway. Jimbo opened a second door...and there it was! ... a *slot machine* with flashing lights, bells, and even music! I had never seen one, other than in the movies or on television. I didn't even know that they were illegal. Jimbo put in a quarter and pulled down the lever. Then I tried it. Within ten minutes we had lost five dollars, four of it mine. That was also my cab fare home.

There was a pencil with a pad of paper near the slot machine, and Jimbo asked me if I wanted to make a bet on the baseball game… and to give him a number. I didn't know what he was talking about, but I gave him the number "seven" anyway. He wrote it down on the pad, tore off the piece of paper, and then disappeared for a couple of minutes. When he returned, he told me that he had placed a two-dollar bet, and that he had covered the two dollars since we had lost mostly my money on the slot machine.

"You're all set."

"What'd you do?"

"I placed a bet with Tiny. If the total runs equal seven for tonight's baseball game, you win."

"How much?" I asked.

"On two bucks, that usually pays about thirty dollars."

"Great!"

"You'll never win… don't get too excited."

I thought to myself that if I'd never win, why did he make the bet?

It was close to nine o'clock, and time for me to figure out how I was going to get home without calling my parents. Tiny was on his way out the front door of the poolroom, so Jimbo ran up to him and asked if we could both get a ride home. I started to shake my head, but within a few minutes, I found myself in a new Lincoln Continental. It was all white with gold trim and had the most comfortable seats on the planet, white leather with crushed velvet… a couch in a car!

Tiny didn't seem so incredibly large in the Lincoln, but I felt very, very small. Jimbo sat in the front seat with Tiny, and I couldn't even see his head. I only lived a few miles away but as the saying goes, we were "worlds apart." My mother saw me get out of the Lincoln and asked who had given me a ride in such an expensive car. I told her that he was a friend of Jimbo's. I knew that if my parents saw me in Tiny's car again, there would be some real explaining to do... but that never happened. The only time I ever saw Tiny after that night was from a distance, and he still looked massive, standing there on the sidewalk in front of the poolroom.

DECISIONS

"You won!"

"What?" I said to Jimbo on the phone the next day.

"You won... the number was seven. Did you see the score of last night's baseball game? It was six to one. That makes seven and you won fifty-two dollars!"

"No way! I thought you said I'd never win... I don't believe it. How did they come up with fifty-two dollars? That's a strange amount to..."

Jimbo interrupted me, "I just spoke with Albie and he's feeling better. Let's go out and spend your fifty-two dollars. I've already picked it up from Tiny."

Later on that day, the three of us went to the amusement park and spent all of my winnings. We went on so many rides that we were feeling nauseous, especially after five pounds of fried dough.

In the evening, we went back to Tiny's place, but he wasn't there. Jimbo said that there was probably a high stakes card game going on in the back room. We decided to walk over to the taxi stand near the horse track because the dispatcher was also a bookie.

For a couple of weeks we bet on the numbers, but after losing about ten times in a row, I decided not to gamble anymore. My parents always gave me an allowance because I didn't work yet, and they were beginning to wonder why I never had any money!

My Ocean City education was broadening from the amusement park and the bowling alley… to the *little casinos* in the back rooms of social clubs, restaurants, and even in a few drug stores. Ocean City was a gambling mecca because of the dog and horse tracks, and gambling was just a natural by-product of always being around the activity. Unfortunately, it also became an obsession for many people... sometimes for entire families.

Other than being where we shouldn't have been on occasion, Albie, Jimbo, and I didn't get into trouble, but we certainly knew it was around. My parents were pretty much unaware of what I was doing, but they did stay in close contact with Albie's parents who kept us to a strict curfew.

The only time that I can ever remember Albie's parents becoming even mildly annoyed with me was because of a "thousand dollar mistake" in judgment on my part. Being fifteen years old, it wasn't *really* my fault… you be the judge… this is what happened: Albie and I loved to play box ball on the beach. Basically you needed four people on a side. With a stick or a shell, we would draw the outline of a box and bases (baseball diamond) on the hard mud near the water. The person at home plate would punch a rubber (pink or pimple) ball on the ground within the box and try to get it past the four infielders of the opposing team. Any ball hit out of the box in the air was an out.

On a hot and steamy summer afternoon, Albie punched a perfect hit that skimmed the hard mud like a hydroplane… and past the fielders. We were having a great game that had lasted more than an hour. As he raced around the box, he sliced the bottom of his foot on a razor clam that must have surfaced from all the foot pressure of everybody running on the same base path. Jimbo was watching from the sea wall and helped me get Albie off the beach and onto the sidewalk, but we couldn't stop the bleeding with a towel or a T-shirt.

Somebody flagged down a police car, and I asked one of the officers to call for an ambulance, which arrived in a few minutes to take Albie to the emergency room. We then ran over to Albie's house and told his parents what had happened. The four of us quickly headed toward the local hospital in his father's car. After driving for about ten minutes, Jimbo and I noticed that the same kind of ambulance that had picked up Albie was just ahead of us. We looked at each other as if to say, "that couldn't be *his* ambulance" but it was. I don't know how they were so slow, or maybe we just reached his parents' house really quickly, but it was very strange to arrive at the hospital *before* the ambulance… and by then, the bleeding had stopped.

When Albie's parents received the bill for one thousand eighteen dollars, I guess they weren't too happy considering that they could have brought him there even faster… and the ambulance ride wasn't covered by insurance because there was "no emergency status" applied to the call. It certainly seemed like an emergency to me! Albie's parents didn't think that they should have had to pay five hundred dollars a stitch. I'm sure that *my* parents picked up the tab on a few dinners after that.

KARMA

In my town, some people would say that Port James had "character" and Ocean City had "characters." Rocco was certainly one of those characters. He would wait at the bus stop or train station and try to scam people for money… via the "shake-down." On any given day, he would walk up to some unsuspecting people and tell them that he had information about their illegal activities or even photos of infidelity. They were completely made up stories, but most people had some personal baggage. I mean who doesn't? Occasionally he would hit pay dirt and continue with his extortion for months. This "business venture" lasted for a couple of years, but eventually Rocco harassed the wrong person.

While Rocco was a wannabe, Sonny was the real thing. He had an "office" at the local diner, and was the main supplier of sports gambling cards. He was also the only "low interest" loan shark around. Sonny really looked the part: He wore a fedora, smoked big cigars, and had fingers the size of bananas; but he wasn't one of those "I'll kill you if you look at me the wrong way" types. He was very personable and really popular with the kids.

Rocco and Sonny crossed paths, and it was too bad for Rocco. In an ironic sense of revenge for the shooting of Debbie's friend, years ago… Jimbo pointed him out to Sonny in the diner after Sonny had begun to ask around if anyone knew a guy named Rocco. Someone with that name had been hassling his niece at the bus stop.

Jimbo had met Sonny at the diner and would sell a few football cards for him. Once in awhile, Albie and I would help Jimbo wash Sonny's car on the weekends for ten dollars. Sonny wasn't a bad guy as far as gangsters go, but Jimbo kept his distance because he knew that Sonny might ask for a favor, and Jimbo didn't want to get into that way of life. He was too smart for that.

Sonny ended up "talking" to Rocco, who then spent a week in the hospital with a concussion and about fifty stitches on the back of his head. His father tried to convince him to become a carpenter and join the union, but eventually Rocco found work making license plates.

……………………………………………………………

Like many beach towns, Ocean City and Port James had designated areas of their sea walls that reflected where certain groups from different neighborhoods, or people from other towns and cities would congregate. There was a lot of drinking going on which constantly led to verbal threats and altercations. Sometimes, there were brutal fights but very rarely a stabbing or a shooting. Guns were for mobsters in those days.

In Ocean City one time, I remember seeing a carload of mini-thugs with baseball bats and tire irons suddenly jump out of an old Chevy and attack a group of wall sitters who weren't bothering anybody. A couple of guys were seriously hurt, and that led to a number of retaliations. Another time I watched two groups of older kids from rival towns walk near each other when some "ethnic slurs" were made. That fight had to broken up by the Metropolitan Police who constantly patrolled the boulevard.

One early evening, Albie and I were hanging out at my sea wall with some friends in Port James when a car drove by and three sets of girls' hands waved to Albie… calling his name as they passed by us. Suddenly they stopped, backed up, and rolled down the window. "Do you guys want to go to a club?" the driver asked. They were definitely a couple of years older than we were. Without really thinking too much about it, we just hopped into the back seat. Albie turned to me and said, "We're going to a club!"

The only clubs that I had ever been to were social clubs and yacht clubs, so that's where I expected us to be going.

I LOVE THE NIGHT LIFE

Being in a car with older girls and going to a nightclub was all new territory for me; I wasn't even sixteen yet. As the car sped off, I noticed that the girls had beer under the back seat, so I thought that for sure we were going to get arrested. Albie told me to relax… that he knew the girls from Ocean City High School. They were seniors.

It was starting to get darker as we pulled into the West End of a neighboring city. Albie's parents were going out with my parents for the evening, which meant that our curfew might be a little later than usual. Darkness approached as the five of us parked in front of an old brick building with a turned off sign that I couldn't read. The girls strolled right into the club, and we followed them.

Nobody asked us for identification; it seemed like the place wasn't quite open. There was a band setting up in a corner across from the bar near a small dance floor, which seemed to have a different kind of wood than the rest of the place. Basically it was a *real* dance floor, and I had never seen one before.

A waiter approached us and asked if we wanted a drink. I was surprised because we really didn't look old enough, but it was fairly dark in there except for some colored lights, flashing wildly around and across the room. Albie and I ordered a "Cape Codder" which tasted more like straight cranberry juice and that was okay with me. I was in a real club… in the city!

There was some loud background music, which was controlled from behind the bar where two bartenders were battling over what radio station to play. They were like a comedy act, and Albie and I were having a good time watching them. Out of the corner of my eye, I noticed something that I had never seen before, anywhere. *Two guys were dancing together.* Now I had seen groups of girls dancing together or even two girls dancing with each other at a party or a wedding reception, but this was a first. With a slight look of "hello reality," Albie turned to me and said, "I think this is a gay bar!"

I replied quickly, "What if someone sees us? They'll think we're gay. Why else would we be here? I'm leaving!"

Albie laughed and answered, "How are you going to get home? Relax… nobody knows us here, and it's dark. Let's hang out and have another drink. We'll find the girls and get a ride back to Ocean City."

"That's fine with me," I said. "The sooner the better… you know I don't think they're putting any alcohol in our drinks, and they haven't even charged us any money for them."

Albie ordered a couple of beers, but the waiter never returned with them. Somebody must have said something to him about us being underage or maybe he just forgot about us.

It could have been from the energy of the place, or just that we felt *older*, but we were having a really good time. Albie and I hooked up with the girls at a booth where they gave us a few sips of their beers. Now, the whole "club" experience was definitely more complete in our minds. The girls asked us what we thought of the place, so we *had* to inform them that it was a "gay bar." They started to giggle and told us that it was cool to be there even though they weren't gay. We didn't question it anymore and they pulled us up on the dance floor. The place was getting very crowded as the music from the band replaced the radio. The group was good, but I think that they were guys dressed up as women. They were called "The Trans" and of course it now makes sense to me... but at the time I thought the name was short for "Trans Ams."

As we were all dancing and goofing around, Albie and I were suddenly facing each other doing a dance step that we copied from the girls. It kind of freaked us out a little bit, and we both decided that it was time to leave. The girls were thinking the same thing because they grabbed our hands like we were their dates… or little children, and we walked out the front door together. There was a huge line that wrapped around the block and it seemed as though everybody was dressed up in some kind of costume. The outside sign lit up the sidewalk and in red script lettering spelled…

DARLINGS.

That was a strange club to go to for a *first time,* but things got even a little crazier. The girls had dropped us off at the corner of the beach near the local strip club. Feeling particularly bold, Albie said that we should go in and check it out. I told him that there was no way we could get in, but he said that Jimbo had shown him a side entrance that the strippers used before they went on stage. It was near the dressing room, and we could slip in from there and go to the side corridor and watch. For more than the second time that night, I was starting to feel a little apprehensive. I had never seen women stripping on a stage (or anywhere else before). Albie and I were able to watch a *show* and stay undetected for about ten minutes until a monster came up to us and threatened to "knock our heads off." We quickly left and headed towards the amusement park to get some pizza, laughing all the way… once we got outside, of course. We had time for one slice before getting back to Albie's house by curfew. Jimbo was waiting on the front porch steps when we got there, and he had a smirk on his face.

"How's the happy couple doing?"

"What?" Albie and I said in unison.

"Yeah, I heard you guys went on a date tonight."

I guess Jimbo had asked around if anyone had seen us, and one of the girls who took us there had told him about the club. Albie and I jumped on his back and tried to wrestle him down, but that was a mistake. He flicked us off like beads of water on wax. Suddenly, approaching headlights flooded the driveway, and a car pulled up next to the house. My parents waved as they went inside with

Albie's folks. We casually waved back and then started the grill to roast some marshmallows "city style."

I learned a couple of things that night: I knew that I was heterosexual, but I also knew that I didn't care if anyone else was... or wasn't.

DINNER AGAIN

When Jimbo invited Albie and me to go to dinner with him at his dad's house, I didn't want to go because I knew that his dad had a serious drinking problem; but living in the same town as his dad, I really *had* to show up. I took the short bus ride there and met Albie and Jimbo outside the house, which was a two family residence and not in very good shape.

I was surprised at how nice Jimbo's dad seemed to be, but his breath definitely smelled like he had drunk a six-pack. He was also lighting up cigarettes without realizing that he had more than one going, which made me a little nervous, but it was kind of funny. His dad was short like Jimbo, but he wasn't muscular at all. The tattoos on his biceps looked like shriveled up inkblots. There wasn't much furniture in the place, but it wasn't *that* bad... considering the circumstances.

His dad placed some beers on the counter and then put them back into the refrigerator as he told us that we were too young to drink. We played cards at the kitchen table while his father tended to a roast beef in the oven, and I was impressed by his dad's knowledge of cooking as he informed us of the different spices that he liked to use. A few minutes later, his dad put some fresh Italian bread on the table, which already had plates and silverware stacked, ready to use.

We set the table and waited... and waited... and waited. Finally his dad took the roast out of the oven. He had also broiled some potatoes and vegetables in the same pan. It looked good and I was hungry. I hadn't eaten too much that day because I had been playing basketball with some friends and then had gone straight to the house.

For no apparent reason, Jimbo's dad began to laugh hysterically and then he just yelled out, "I'm on the wagon! No hard stuff today! Yeah!"

Jimbo looked at me and said that it was time to go, but I was really hungry and wanted to eat. I wanted some of that roast. It smelled good! I looked at Albie, but I could tell that he wasn't too committed to the meal anymore. Jimbo's dad got up and made his way over to the oven, but as he turned around to come back to the table, he slipped on a little grease that had spilled on the floor, and he fell against the stove. I thought that he was knocked out or passed out... and then to our amazement, he just got up like nothing had happened and started talking about football.

Jimbo quickly attended to his dad, who began to scream at the top of his lungs, "I'll cut the roast! I'll cut the roast!" The guy was inebriated... loaded! He tried to whack Jimbo on the back of the head... when he suddenly grabbed the roast with one hand. "Catch the pass!" he yelled. "Catch the pass!" He just whipped the roast across the room... right out the window... total insanity... but we couldn't help but laugh.

Albie and I left and waited for Jimbo downstairs; then the three of us walked a couple of miles to my house to get something to eat. My parents weren't home, but there were leftovers in the fridge, so we ate some chicken and dessert.

Jimbo explained to us that his family had fallen apart a long time ago from the drinking, and his mother had moved to Ocean City so that she could be closer to her own family. It was difficult to raise two children as a single parent. Jimbo would visit with his father and straighten out the house, but he knew that it was almost a hopeless situation… even for "The Hulk."

CONCLUSION

Drawing by Mark DellaPenna

That day at his dad's house was the last time that we hung out together that particular summer, but we would have many other memorable times over the next few years. In thinking back about my childhood in Port James, I was comfortable and secure; my friends were predictable and for the most part, it was almost literally smooth sailing from yacht clubs to college courses; but the education that I received in Ocean City helped me to navigate through some of *life's* most difficult challenges.

Jimbo's father continued in his self-destructive alcoholic way of life. Although Jimbo's mother encouraged Jimbo to maintain some contact with his dad, especially during the holidays, things continued to spiral down until his father eventually shot himself and died a few days later. Jimbo told me that his dad had been looking for him... the day he committed suicide. Jimbo was sure that he wanted to "take him with him," to get back at his mother.

Ocean City kids were hardened by their circumstances and functioned in more of a "survival" mode than the way we lived in Port James. Somewhere in between, I developed a broader sense of the world around me... and I was fortunate enough to have developed two meaningful and lasting friendships.

These days, whenever I see Albie or Jimbo, we laugh about those years, and they always tell me that I should write a story or a book... so guys, here it is... somewhere in between! If I've left anything out or changed some of the facts or details, let me know. We'll fix it for the movie!

"Brian"

One early Sunday morning as I was driving near South Station in Boston, I noticed a familiar walk at a distance. There was only one person who walked as if he were leaning back at an obtuse angle; it had to be Brian. I immediately stopped the car and saw that it was, indeed, my old friend. Upon recognizing me, he burst into a huge smile and enthusiastically shook my hand. It had been almost fifteen years since we had last seen each other.

Many years earlier in September of 1969, I arrived at the University of Massachusetts in Amherst as a college freshman. I lived in a so-called experimental dormitory known as "Project 10" which was located in the Southwest campus. It was intended to be a progressive and communal living experience for freshmen and sophomore students; however, other than having some of our classes in the dormitory, there was almost nothing progressive or communal about it. During my four years at college, I somehow managed to obtain a reasonably traditional education despite a student political climate that was incredibly volatile. Nixon was president, and the Vietnam War continued to rage. Anti-war protests, rock concerts and everything else that went with them totally dominated our cultural scene. The only positive experience that I had from living in "Project 10" was that I met Brian and Vincent during our first semester, and we became instant friends as well as roommates for all of our undergraduate college years.

After graduating in 1973, we went our separate ways, but the feeling of what we had shared during those times was part of me, and I'm sure that some of the feeling remained with them too. Unfortunately, the hedonistic days of Disco supplanted the idealism of Woodstock, and our friendship was never recaptured. Just recently, I've come to a personal revelation that this time period of social change and revolution may have been more of a periscope into the future and not just a reflection of the past.

Although Brian studied psychology in college, he was a very talented artist who decided to pursue his natural ability in drawing and become an architect. It was right around the time that he was thinking of going to graduate school for architecture, that he informed some of his friends that he was gay. This was quite a shock to me because I could not understand how a close heterosexual friend of mine could actually go through a process of sexual metamorphosis, and it was not a matter of preference in life-style for Brian as some people may have thought; he was just gay, and somehow he figured it out.

As Brian became more immersed into the gay culture, we no longer clicked. It seemed as though he became a different person because of his sexuality, or maybe we both just changed. I, myself, unfortunately went into a ten year retrograde throughout the mid-seventies and early eighties and actually became part of a lost generation of one. I could have used Brian's friendship and Vincent's too, but it just wasn't meant to be.

When I saw Brian again on that Sunday morning, it was as if no time had passed between us. We made plans to have lunch, and we got together a few days later at Quincy Marketplace. He showed me his apartment in Harbor Towers and talked about his work as an architect. He was doing very well, but the AIDS epidemic had taken its toll upon his psyche because many of his friends were sick or had already died from the treacherous disease.

Brian was not infected with the virus, but he told me that HIV was not going to deter his search for new potential relationships. He asked about Vincent and suggested that the three of us get together, but we never did. Brian had always been reluctant to reveal his sexuality to Vincent for some reason, but sexuality was never an issue for Vincent. I think the only reason that Brian felt more comfortable with me on that level was that after college, he had worked for my band to make some extra money, and it was during this time that things began to change for him. I was aware of it because we both lived at the band house and were still close. I remember asking Brian about his sexual transformation because he had dated many different women during his years in college and never seemed to have any inclination towards men. It just seemed so unbelievable to me.

A couple of years passed after having lunch and spending the day with Brian, and I happened to see Vincent during a Thanksgiving dinner at a function facility owned by his family. We talked about the three of us going out, but once again it just never happened. A few months later, I received a telephone call from one of Brian's oldest friends. He said that he was calling because he was curious about what I had been doing all these years. We talked for a few minutes, and then I asked him if he had seen Brian recently. He nonchalantly responded, "Oh, he's dead." He told me that Brian's father had cared for Brian during the final stages of AIDS and that Brian had suffered greatly from its effects. At that moment, I don't know if I was more devastated from the news or from the way it was delivered. Brian's friend, who at one time had been a good acquaintance of mine, must have been incredibly traumatized from Brian's death and was unable to communicate his grief in a normal way because it was one of the strangest phone calls that I have ever received. I went to see Vincent to tell him, and he was very upset to hear the tragic news about Brian.

Years later, I called Vincent and invited him to lunch. We had a few laughs especially because it was a cash only place, and I was expecting to pay by credit card. As we talked about our life altering experiences from 1969 to 1973, Vincent said that he wished that he could hear Brian's voice just one more time. It was a difficult moment for both of us; we missed him. After a toast to Brian with a glass of wine, I suggested that the two of us take a day trip and visit our old stomping grounds in Amherst. Vincent seemed more amused than interested and said that it would be difficult for him to get away, although he often thought about going back for a visit. I wrote him a short note to try to convince him that it was only one day out of our lives, but we never did make that trip. It just wouldn't be the same, and we both knew it.

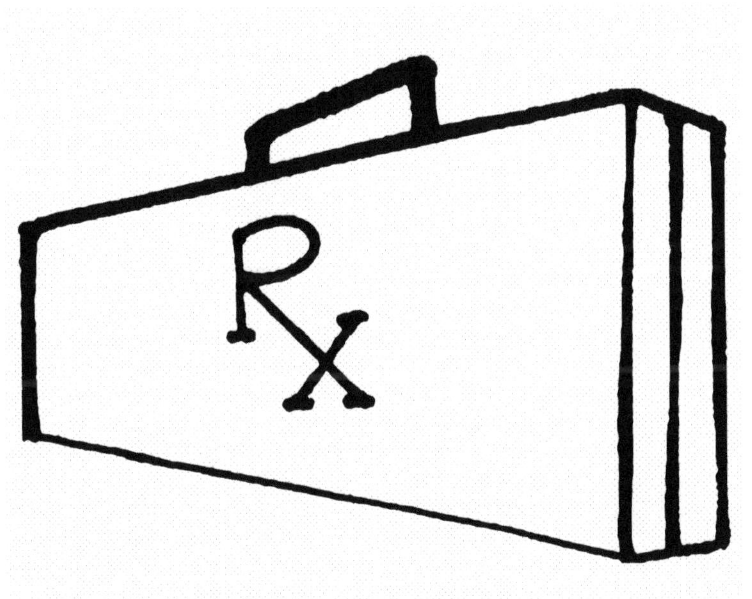

"The Taste of Medicine"

Cameron's briefcase was missing, and most of the people who worked with Cameron were not unhappy about his misfortune because he was not very well liked, and with good reason. Although he presented as outgoing and compassionate to his superiors, Cameron was anything but that, and his cleverness was not to be denied. He basically surrounded himself with people who owed him favors, or new employees who were eager to succeed within the corporate continuum. No one would have suspected that Peggy, a college student and temporary employee, would be the one who could disrupt Cameron's world, but she had, indeed, taken his briefcase. It was during one of Cameron's verbally abusive tirades directed at one of Peggy's friends who also worked for the temporary agency, that Peggy decided to do it.

The briefcase was really not much larger than a purse, and Peggy just put it under her coat on the way to her lunch break. It was easy to do because Cameron was always leaving his personal things around the office, as if to mark off his territory. Peggy felt exhilarated, like a character from "Mission Impossible." After stashing the briefcase in her car, she ate lunch by herself and then returned to work. Cameron seemed almost frantic as he walked up and immediately questioned her as to whether or not she had seen any strangers in the office. She told him that she hadn't seen anyone who was unfamiliar and asked him if there was a problem. Walking away from her, Cameron yelled back without turning his head, "Yes, there's a problem!" Peggy looked around the office and noticed that everyone was smiling and making little remarks about Cameron's missing briefcase. He was not a popular man. Peggy felt some remorse for what she had done; however, she thought that people like Cameron bordered on ruthless and just needed to be stopped. He didn't play fair, so maybe she didn't have to either.

That evening, Peggy stared at the briefcase on her night table as she listened to the news and ate some dinner. She thought about opening the briefcase but instead decided to return it. The whole idea of what she had done now seemed foolish. Arriving an hour early the next morning, Peggy looked around to make sure that she was alone and then knocked on the men's room door. Once convinced that nobody was in there, she placed the briefcase behind a toilet and quickly left. Peggy then exited the building and called the answering service to let them know that she would be late for work. After waiting for almost an hour at a nearby coffee shop, she returned to the office and noticed a police officer in the hallway. She asked someone about what was going on, and she was told that Cameron's missing briefcase had been found. Apparently, he wanted it dusted for fingerprints, but the police said that they did not have time to deal with nuisance cases, and they were just in the process of leaving. At that moment, Peggy felt the blood return to her face.

Cameron was laughing as he appeared at her desk later on that day. He said that he had just heard a joke from the president of the company and wondered if Peggy would like to hear it. She listened but did not laugh too much even though it was almost funny. She had observed from the beginning that Cameron would try to make his little connections with people through his jokes and innuendos, and she was not going to let him even think about that possibility with her. Feeling her disinterest, Cameron was no longer in a laughing mood, and he mentioned to her that the temporary agency had asked him to do an evaluation of her job performance in the company. He added that over the next few weeks, he would be working very closely with her. Peggy did not respond to him, but she was concerned about what he had said. This assignment paid well, and it complemented her college schedule, perfectly.

The next day, everyone was talking about going out that evening, but Peggy was preoccupied with trying to speak with someone at the temporary agency to find out about the pending evaluation. When she finally reached a supervisor who knew about procedural issues and follow-up, she was told that the agency evaluated its own temporary employees and would never request that a client company perform any kind of evaluation. Peggy was relieved, but she was also angry because it appeared as though Cameron may have fabricated the entire thing to gain some kind of psychological advantage over her.

Peggy had no intention of participating in the office after-hours festivities for that evening, and she also had some studying to do for her classes. On her way out of the office at the end of the day, Peggy eyed Cameron's favorite gold and silver pen, which was on the reception desk near the entrance. She discreetly slipped it into her pocket and walked out the door. It was time for another dose.

"Ant Lessons"

When I first began my search for enlightenment at the age of twenty-four, it was basically a conscious decision, on my part, to try and become a better person. Reading some philosophy was going to be one vehicle for me to approach that state of being. I remember going on a vacation to visit two acquaintances of mine, who were living in Camden, Maine. After spending a couple of days with them, it was time for me to go off by myself and begin my reading. The author was a contemporary philosopher whose book I had purchased before the trip and whose name I do not remember.

On that important day, when I would begin my intellectual and emotional encounter with philosophy, I drove around for a while to try and find the ideal location for this experience. Finally, I saw the perfect grassy spot on a protruding cliff with an unobstructed view of the ocean. With book in hand, I was ready to begin my philosophical journey, while relating to nature at the same time.

After walking up a dirt path, I then relaxed in some meadow-like grass and stared out at the ocean. I almost felt smug, like I was privy to the secrets of truth and was going to receive many incredible insights that would impact my life and even transform my soul! As I began to read the first page, my mind immediately started to wander, and then I luckily happened upon a few inspirational words, which vaguely referred to the sanctity of life. It was right at this time that I detected a large ant carrying a morsel of food. The insect was within elbow's length, so without really thinking, I lopped off its head with my thumbnail and index finger. Another ant appeared, and I quickly lopped off its head too.

Now once being a young boy doing battle with insects and rodents, I could almost rationalize this action, but as an emerging adult, I now had to ask myself the question: How could I be reading about the sanctity of life and do what I just did—twice? In that moment, I had begun to realize that those ants represented something far greater than two "meaningless" little creatures, and I could not go back and fix what I had done because they were no longer alive. Strictly in terms of life and death, I had ended two life forces for no apparent reason other than...they were there, and they were just insects. What was I thinking or not thinking? I did not feel like reading anymore, so I returned to my car and drove for about four hours until I made it back to the Boston area to spend the rest of the vacation at my own shoreline.

I never really thought about the incident until a number of years later when I was going to eliminate a centipede that had unknowingly entered my domain. I suddenly had a flashback to that moment on the Maine seacoast, and it instantly changed me.

Although I haven't always adhered to my personal goal of respecting the sanctity of life for all creatures like mosquitoes, termites, or countless other insects, every time I think about *slap, swat,* or *squish,* I pause, and those two little ants appear in my mind. With a little ingenuity and some patience, I usually find that there is some other way.

"A Night Out"

The band had just finished its last set, and the musicians gathered around the table to pay their tab. There wasn't much of a crowd that night, but the group still had a good time playing some of the new original songs that they had just written. During the early seventies, there weren't too many other funk-fusion bands around that wrote their own material, and even though some of the musicians in the band weren't really that proficient on their instruments, they were innovative songwriters. As they discussed the evening's performance over a few beers, Danny, the keyboard player, noticed two men in their early twenties who were staring at him from across the room. When he glanced back over at their table a few minutes later, they were gone.

The next day, Danny was awakened by a telephone call from a person who identified himself as Tom Porter from Springfield. Tom said that he was also a keyboard player, and he had seen the group the night before. He had gotten the telephone number of the band house from one of the road crew. After speaking for a few moments and giving his critique of the band, he then asked Danny if they could meet and exchange some musical ideas. Danny was open to the idea, but considering all the expensive equipment that the band kept on the premises, it was unlikely that he was going to invite some stranger to come there for any reason. Not to be impolite, Danny asked Tom to call back some time in the future, and possibly they could make arrangements to get together and jam.

That afternoon, Danny and the bass player, Rico, met for lunch. They were the leaders of the group as well as best friends and would meet during the afternoons, a few days a week, to discuss band business. Danny mentioned the phone call, and they both agreed that they should be somewhat cautious about having strangers visit the band house. Over lunch, they discussed the music set list for that evening and walked around Amherst for a couple of hours.

Later on in the day when Danny arrived home, the phone rang. It was Tom Porter again. Having just spoken to him, Danny was surprised to hear his voice. Tom asked where the band was playing that night, so Danny told him that they were going to be at the Rusty Nail in Sunderland. Tom said that he would be there and introduce himself, and Danny suggested that Tom should drop by the stage.

The night at the club was fairly typical. There were about a hundred people having a good time, dancing and listening to the music. As Danny left the stage after the first set, he thought that he recognized two faces in the crowd from the night before in Springfield. They were seated at a table in the back of the room. After finishing a long second set, Danny went outside to get some air and talk with some musician friends who were off for the night and had come to hear the group. Tom Porter never showed up.

For the next two weeks, the band went on a mini-tour in Maine. They played at a number of colleges on the coast and worked at a ski resort. Primarily a local band, not many people outside of the Amherst and Northampton area really knew of them; however, the group usually received a good response. When Danny returned to the band house in Sunderland after his two weeks on the road, there were a few messages from some nightclubs, a college, a booking agent, and a message from Tom Porter. Danny returned his call.

Tom was very persuasive about getting together that night and said that he could really "show Danny some things on the keyboard." Reluctantly, Danny agreed to meet with him at the band house and gave him directions. Tom never made it.

He did not hear from Tom until a few months later when Tom phoned one evening. He asked Danny if they could meet at an apartment where one of Tom's friends lived. He said it would just be a little night out among some musicians. Danny knew the location of the apartment complex because it was always being advertised for rentals in the local newspaper. He agreed to finally meet with Tom, and that evening he found the place easily enough.

Tom Porter opened the door and introduced himself as he began to play something on an acoustic guitar. It was obvious to Danny that Tom was a novice, yet Tom mentioned that although he was a keyboard player, he also had been playing guitar for more than twelve years. Danny wondered about that. Tom introduced his three friends, and Danny thought that he recognized at least one of them from the club in Springfield or the Rusty Nail. He wasn't exactly sure. Tom then suggested that they all drive to the University together and use one of the music department's practice rooms, which had a piano. It seemed like a good idea to everyone.

As the five of them piled into his car, Danny was suddenly overcome with a feeling of intense trepidation. Questions suddenly arose in his mind. How could Tom Porter be so bad on the guitar after playing the instrument for twelve years? How did he end up alone with four strangers in his car? The whole scene was just wrong!

Before even leaving the parking lot, he felt his body rise as he opened the car door, and then he just took off into the night's blackness. He ran as fast as he could through an open field. Stopping to rest only for a moment, he listened but detected no voices behind him; nobody was following him as he had anticipated, and Danny was relieved.

From the local diner, he telephoned the band house and the road manager came and picked him up. Not that it was unusual, but Danny realized that there wasn't anybody who had known where he was that night. As they drove to the apartment complex to get Danny's car, the two of them were laughing at the thought of Danny running for his life through some little field. It must have been quite a sight. Danny was anxious to apologize for acting so irrationally. It was embarrassing, but he didn't really care that much. The whole night was strange. Upon arriving at the apartment complex, they proceeded to ring the doorbell of the apartment, but nobody answered. They went in through the main entrance and knocked on the door of the apartment, but nobody seemed to be there. Finally, Danny turned the doorknob and gently pushed open the unlocked door. The light was still on, but the place was empty except for the real estate section of the newspaper spread out on the kitchen counter. There was an advertisement for the apartment complex, and circled on the page was the number of that very apartment—listed as vacant. Danny never heard from Tom Porter again.

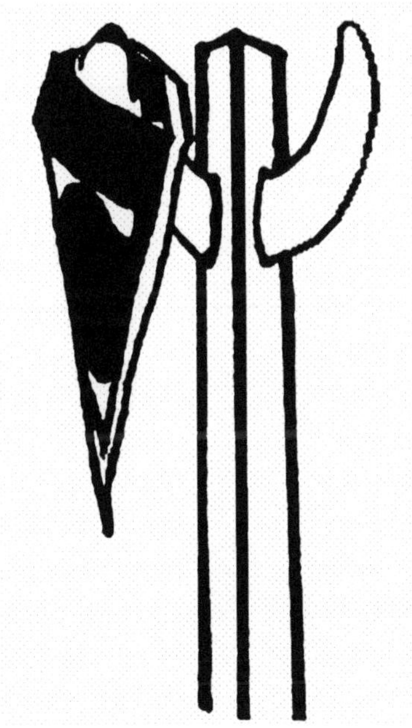

"The End of Superman"

It was any hot day in July of 1958, and the burning sand scorched our little feet, which made us wonder why our mothers didn't situate the beach chairs closer to the cooler hard sand near the water. Most families would arrive at the beach just after 8:00 a.m. and stay the entire day, sometimes until after 7:00 p.m. My mother would always pack a wonderful lunch of sandwiches, drinks, grapes, cherries and cookies. We lived close to the beach on a side street that was perpendicular to the shore drive known as "The Crest." Years later, our little town would become well known during the 1980 Olympics when a hometown hero scored the winning goal against the Russians.

During that summer in 1958, I was totally consumed with the most famous person in not just the world, but also in the universe. He was more than a man, and he epitomized everything that I aspired to be, living in my heart as a symbol of "truth, justice, and the American way." Whenever I was at the beach during that summer, I couldn't wait to put a towel around my neck and run into the wind. My towel would then blow like a cape—like the cape of Superman. Superman was not just some fictitious character on television played by George Reeves, nor was he just a comic book hero from the hundreds of comic books that we would read at the local barbershop on Shirley Street. Superman was like a god, and he was far more impressive than any Atlas or Nike missile of the Cold War.

Every Superman wanted a Lois Lane, but I was lucky enough to have Superwoman. She was six years old and my first girlfriend. She would come for the summer with her family, like many other families who escaped the oppressive city heat, and they would live in a cottage near our house for two months. Our parents remained very good friends throughout the years.

One of my favorite memories of that summer was going to a restaurant known as The Spray, which was at the top of the street and directly across from the beach. We would sit on the sea wall and feast on fried clams, shrimp rolls, hot dogs, burgers, and fries. At least once a week, we would also go digging for clams and then steam them up with some butter and salt. Nearby where we would dig, the jetties were almost totally covered with mussels, which looked disgusting to us. If only we had known that great meals were at our fingertips, and it is only now that I understand why the seagulls loved them so much.

Of course, like in most towns, the ice cream man would visit our streets on a daily basis. Occasionally, the fruit man would drive his truck up and down the streets during the afternoon while his brother walked very slowly behind the truck calling out, "Peaches...peaches." He had a booming monotone voice and a huge overhanging belly. We really enjoyed imitating him and how he would hold out the "pee…" sound in peaches.

Another vivid memory for me was how the sun showers seemed to be so much more intense than they are today. The sky would darken while we were at the beach, and then everyone would fold up their beach chairs and leave en masse. The place would become deserted within a few minutes, and then an incredible downpour would ensue. When the rains ended, everyone would return to the beach and just gaze at the rainbow, which filled the sky from one end of the horizon to the other. Although we were disappointed about having to leave the beach because of a storm, the rainbows would always make it worth it when we returned.

On a typical day, something happened to me that would probably seem insignificant to most people–to most people who were not six years old. I had just come out of the water with blue lips and a shivering body so that I could change into something dry, and my mother held a beach towel around me as I slipped into another bathing suit. I then put on my cape (towel) and ran close to the water's edge to build a sand castle with the other kids. We would dig underground tunnels to let the water into the moat of the castle, and then control the water's flow until the inevitable collapse and final destruction of our creation as the high tide came in. With my cape blowing in the ocean filled breeze, I felt like Superman. I *was* Superman. The blazing sun warmed my bones, and it's a feeling that I can still remember after all these years.

I ran back to our area in the dry hot sand, and a woman in our group of families was talking to my mother. Apparently, this woman had said to my mother that I was "some kind of Superman with my skinny little legs." For the first time, I heard an opinion of me other than from my own internal perspective, and it was given by someone from outside of the family, which made it even more traumatic. Her comment made me feel embarrassed, almost humiliated. Of course I knew that I really wasn't Superman, but why did she have to say something like that? Why did she have to say anything about me at all?

From that day forward, my mother would question me as to why I refused to even acknowledge that woman or her daughter, who also happened to be friends with Superwoman. The woman could not understand why I would not even look in her direction whenever she was close by. What she did not realize was that when I did look at her, it was painful because I saw myself as she saw me—a vulnerable little boy with tears in his eyes, and not Superman at all. I really felt no true animosity towards her, yet what *she* may have learned from the experience was that this Superman really did have some powers—including the power to hold back affection. Still, I never put on my cape again.

"For Better or For Worse"

He had only been to one bachelor party in his life, and that was enough for him. The strangest part about the party was that despite knowing the guys for many years, he discovered that there were things about them that he did not know at all. For instance, who would think that two lines of ten married men would quickly form at the bedroom doors of two hookers in a nasty Cape Cod motel as part of the celebration? It wasn't important that the hookers were extremely unattractive, but that was the case. Of course, he just had to ask one of the hookers if she had ever thought about doing something else for a living, and that was the first time that he had ever heard about someone trying to earn money this way to get through college. It probably was a common theme among some hookers who were trying to better themselves.

Arriving late for the party, he was expecting some music, maybe a poker game, Chinese food, a few toasts, and possibly a trip to the local strip club at the end of the night for those who wanted to go. Now as a child of the sixties and seventies, he was no prude, but what he experienced that night was enough to make him question the whole concept of marriage vows. He walked over to the little buffet table, made a sandwich for himself, and said hello to a few people.

Before the hookers arrived, someone asked him if he wanted to take a chance on a raffle, so he handed over a dollar and asked what the raffle was for. Apparently, it was a drawing to get twenty minutes with one of the hookers. He didn't ask for the dollar back and quickly offered it as a donation. What happened next was like a scene from a double x-rated movie that most people would never want to see. Suddenly appearing at the door were the two young women who seemed to really like each other and began to show the group, the total extent of their mutual affection. Ultimately the groom joined in with them, right in front of his own father and three brothers who watched approvingly. Now that was one liberal family, but there was more than one person who viewed this spectacle with one eye shut and the other eye squinted.

The girls circulated among the crowd to discuss various price structures and services. As the lines formed and the girls retired to their bedrooms, he sat down on the floor, leaned against the wall and drank a beer. It tasted flat.

A final lasting image for him was not even from the bachelor party at all, and may or may not have actually occurred. He really didn't know because he wasn't invited to the Hyannis wedding, but this is what he thought had probably taken place. Once again, the guys were back in line, joking around with each other and laughing. Standing next to each one of them was a loving wife or girlfriend.

Together, they would wait patiently until they finally had the opportunity to extend their very best wishes to their friend, the groom, and to the groom's lucky new bride.

"A Simple Solution"

Simon was a good boy. That's what my wife Beth said. He was a really good boy, but he still ended up on cat 'death row' with three days to live. Now cat death row, also known as euthanasia, is similar to our human death row; however, it is much quicker and with only a minimum of paper work.

Simon, a black cat with a swath of white on his leg and underside, lived next door to us. He was a twelve-year-old cat whose owner had recently discovered that her young child was allergic to him; consequently, Simon was not allowed into their house anymore. The adjustment was not that drastic for him, at least in the warm weather. Occasionally he would visit us, much to the annoyance of our own neurotic housecat, but Simon never stayed more than a few moments. He just preferred to be outside most of the time. Simon was a good boy.

It started to bother me that this nice little cat really did not have a home, and I thought about a local animal shelter from where we had adopted our cat. I was a regular contributor there because in their newsletters, they always mentioned that they never destroyed their resident animals. I was impressed. The logical solution was to bring Simon to the animal shelter so that a caring family could adopt him. Beth liked the idea, as did Simon's owner. The next day I found Simon in the backyard and forced him into a pet carrier. I was amazed by his gentleness in that he didn't even try to scratch me despite his intense resistance. Simon was a good boy.

We arrived at the animal shelter, and I described Simon to one of the shelter's volunteers. She immediately told me that he was too old to be adopted. She said that they only accepted neutered or spayed cats three years old or less with all their shots. I became incensed. "What do you mean?" I asked. "I'm a regular contributor to this shelter, and my cat needs to be adopted!" She was adamant in her refusal. I stormed out and told her not to ever send me another solicitation. I'm sure that she thought I was unstable. I returned to my car and peered at Simon through the rear window. He seemed content enough in the cat carrier, but I was fuming. As we drove down the highway, I noticed a sign for the Animal Rescue League. We went in and were greeted by two people at the front desk. They were very polite and professional, but it soon became obvious that "animal rescue" actually meant something quite different. Just a few minutes later, I left the facility without Simon. Someone said to me that she was sorry as I walked away with my head down, visibly upset.

During the ride home, I kept thinking about how endearing it was when Simon would scratch at the back door, looking for food or just to say hello. I thought ahead to Friday when he would be put to sleep. For three days, Simon would be alone in a strange place with unfamiliar cats that were awaiting the same fate. I thought to myself that Friday was still three days away, and I should put Simon out of my mind. I also decided to tell Beth that Simon was safe at the shelter.

As soon as Beth arrived home and walked through the door, I immediately revealed the truth to her: Simon was not at the shelter, but instead was at the end of the line.

She responded by saying that Simon was a good boy, and how awful it must be for him to be in a strange place. I told her that I really didn't know what had happened. My intention was to find him a better home, but somehow I had lost sight of that and just found the simple solution. We both agreed that Simon would probably not like my simple solution. Then Beth said, "We have to go get him!" We called the Animal Rescue League, and they told us that he was still there, and very much alive. It was such a relief to see him again, and he looked at me almost as if to ask, "What took you so long?" On the ride home, we stopped at the local pet store to get some additional cat food and a brush for him.

For the past few months, we have been taking care of Simon. He is well fed and brushed every day. Ironically the pet carrier, which is now situated on our back porch, is where he naps. I doubt that he would have ever gone into it if he hadn't gotten used to it during our little ride together in the country, but that fact does little to assuage my guilt. Our cat still avoids him; however, she does accept his presence because even she knows that Simon is a good boy. He is a very good boy.

"Pencil Me In"

Thomas was an industrial arts teacher at a private school near Cambridge. He had met Lydia on the bus. Each day she would sit near him, and he noticed that even when other seats were available, she chose to find a seat that was close to where he was sitting. Finally, they began to talk, and after a short while, they met for coffee. Lydia was a nurse at a hospital not too far from Harvard Square. She loved to watch the street vendors, or shop around at used clothing stores. She definitely had a flair for the unconventional. Thomas was more conservative; however, his off beat humor intrigued her.

Both of them were in their mid-twenties and made an attractive couple. After a couple of months of dating, Thomas asked Lydia to move in with him. He lived in a converted garage owned by his family, and he had done major renovations including the building of a kitchen, a huge loft, and a spiral staircase. Some of his students would help him do welding after school, and he would pay them for their efforts. It was a good opportunity for the students to refine their skills while making some money, and Thomas was able to use the shop area for his own projects.

Lydia specialized in orthopedic nursing. She loved to swim and dreamed about having her own Olympic size pool one day. She had two sisters who were also nurses, and they were all very dedicated to the profession. Sometimes Lydia had to work very late into the night, and Thomas always waited up. He would read or keep busy with the renovations on the garage, which was beginning to look more like a little chalet. Lydia had been really comfortable living with her roommate in Cambridge, but she was beginning to feel like this was her new home.

Thomas was a very good cook. His cousin was a chef in a downtown Boston restaurant, and that's where he learned some of his cooking skills. Lydia was also good in the kitchen, especially at baking. Thomas loved her specialty breads, particularly her wheat bread with sun dried tomatoes and sunflower seeds, which they would sometimes have as an entire meal with a bottle of wine.

Things seemed to be as good as either one of them could want in a relationship. On weekends, Lydia would visit her friends in Cambridge and then occasionally visit her parents and nieces on the South Shore. Thomas' family owned an unusual antique shop, and his three brothers and sister worked there. Thomas would drop by quite often; however, during the weekend mornings, he would work private jobs to supplement his teaching income. Most of his customers were people who knew him from his family's business. Thomas was very skilled and actually had a waiting list for both interior and exterior design and construction work.

Saturday afternoons and evenings belonged to the two of them if she wasn't on call for a weekend shift or if Thomas' work did not extend past the morning hours. Together, they would take long walks. Both of them loved to go to the movies or visit a museum, and they really enjoyed old bookstores and used furniture places. They would spend quite a bit of time in Davis Square just looking around and then maybe go dancing. Thomas loved to dance, and Lydia used to laugh at his goofy antics on the dance floor.

Both Thomas and Lydia were predictable to each other. That is what made them feel so comfortable together; so when Thomas was offered a job in Pennsylvania from a resume that he had sent almost a year prior to meeting her, there was no doubt in Lydia's mind that he would turn it down. Their relationship was moving along in such a positive direction. Thomas went for the job interview, and he met with a group of investors who were forming a large construction company that was going to specialize in merging classic and modern design for new houses. It was precisely what Thomas had presented in his portfolio. They offered him the job immediately after meeting with him.

He struggled about the best way to tell Lydia because he knew there was no good way. She sensed it as soon as he walked through the door. He basically told her that it was a new and different opportunity, and teaching industrial arts was just no longer challenging. For the past two years, he had been enjoying his weekend jobs more than working at the school. That told him something, and that's why he responded to the opportunity when he saw it in the newspaper.

Although she was very disappointed about his decision, she did not let him know it. She tried to be supportive and after all, Thomas would be earning almost three times the amount of money that he was making right now. There was no company car yet, but that was in the works. Lydia was surprised that Thomas seemed to be so impacted by the financial potential. She had never seen that side of him before. Thomas had never seen that side of himself, and it was exciting. They decided that Lydia should still live at his place, and they would try to see each other on weekends whenever possible.

Thomas gave notice to the school with about a month left during the summer vacation. He was offered a leave of absence, which Thomas decided to accept. He was a valuable asset to their community, and they would welcome him back if there was a position available.

Thomas asked Lydia if she would consider joining him in Pennsylvania. He was sure that there were many nursing opportunities that were available in some of the local hospitals. When he mentioned nursing homes, Lydia just shook her head and smiled because she had done too many hours in those kinds of settings long before she had become a nurse. Each of them wondered privately if it was the end of what they had together or whether or not they could build something else with this new arrangement.

When Thomas arrived in Pennsylvania, the last thing on his mind was finding another woman, but that's exactly what he did. Ann was a strong force in the new company. They were using her ideas almost exclusively, and Thomas was very impressed with her creative input and business savvy. In terms of the design work, which needed to be varied so that the houses did not resemble each other too much on the exterior, Thomas and Ann were totally on the same page. In fact they were already at the point where they were finishing each other's sentences during board meetings. Within a short period of time, they made a great team in and out of the office.

Lydia made the decision that she wanted to be with Thomas. Their long distance phone calls were no longer the marathon conversations that had taken place during the first two weeks of their separation, and she was lonely without him. She called Thomas to tell him that she was thinking of joining him, and he responded enthusiastically.

Lydia gave notice at the hospital and then informed Thomas' family that she would be leaving to join Thomas. Everyone was very excited and the word marriage was even brought up by someone in the family. Lydia just laughed and said that she wasn't quite ready for that, and it was not a good idea to project too far into the future. The night before she was to leave for Pennsylvania, all of her belongings were packed and ready to be shipped. Her friends from the hospital unit were having a little party for her at one of their favorite spots in Central Square. As she waited for the cab to take her there, that's when the phone call from Thomas came; he told her that it was over.

Lydia moved back in with her former roommate. There would be three people living there now, so a small den area was converted into a third bedroom for Lydia. She left the few things behind that she and Thomas had purchased together.

As things settled down after the devastating phone call, Lydia needed to channel her energy in a new direction, and she decided to become a swim instructor to train young challenged athletes for the Special Olympics. Swimming was such a passion for Lydia, and she would devote many hours at the pool with her young special athletes. She also began to form new acquaintances and started dating another volunteer who was a physical therapist. They had a lot in common, but that didn't necessarily make for great conversation, and Lydia broke it off after a few months.

Thomas still thought about Lydia and never told Ann about her. He was continuing to do very well designing houses and supervising some of the construction. He and Ann even discussed going into business as a separate entity from the parent corporation, but the timing of such a venture would not be appropriate. In terms of their living situation, Thomas thought that it was impractical for them to maintain two apartments since they were basically living together, but they never moved in together because Ann thought it would give an appearance of impropriety.

Thomas decided to go back to Boston for a visit. It had been almost a year since moving to Pennsylvania and seeing his family. Ann wanted to visit her family who lived in Southern California, and she also wanted to attend her tenth year high school reunion. It was the perfect opportunity for both of them to take a break. Everything had happened so quickly.

When Thomas arrived in Boston, he waited about two days and then called Lydia. When she heard his voice on the telephone, she said nothing. He asked her about how she had been doing; once again she said nothing. Lydia had rehearsed this phone call in her mind over and over again, but now that it was actually happening, she had nothing to say because she had so much to say. Where could she begin? He had totally betrayed her. It wasn't the ending of the relationship or whether or not he became involved with someone else, it was much deeper than that. Lydia had trusted him on another level, a spiritual level. She had let all her defenses come down for Thomas. She wondered how she could have been so wrong about his character, his essence. How could she say all this right now? Lydia just told him that she had to go and hung up the phone.

As Thomas was going to dial her number again, the phone rang; it was Ann. She told him that her high school reunion was boring, and she missed him. Thomas said that he missed her too, but privately he wasn't so sure that he meant Lydia and not Ann. He asked her when she was going back to Pennsylvania, and there was silence on the other end of the line. She told him that she didn't think that she wanted to go back East unless things changed; it was the "whole gig" as she put it. Thomas couldn't believe what he was hearing. She was the rising star in the company. He asked her if there was a problem, and she said that she wasn't satisfied with the financial arrangement anymore. Thomas wondered why she had never mentioned anything about it until now. Ann then asked him if he would like to fly out to California, and they could talk about her plans. Thomas said that he would call her back and let her know.

Thomas did not go to California to see Ann. The next day he decided to visit the school. He said hello to some of his former students and a few of his teacher friends. He didn't stay long; it was no longer his scene. A few of the staff commented on his new style of dress, and Thomas just laughed, but he did like the result of Ann's influence upon his wardrobe. Thomas thought about trying to see Lydia. The hospital was only a mile or so from the school, which had been such a convenient part of them living together. He had forgotten about that. Thomas phoned the hospital and was able to reach her. Lydia was intent upon telling him to never call her again, but she needed to say other things first, so she agreed to meet him at The

Bombay Club in Harvard Square. Both of them loved Indian food.

When Thomas arrived at the restaurant, Lydia was waiting outside on the steps. They hugged for a moment and then went inside. She was much more upbeat than he thought she would be, and Thomas was surprised. They talked about their work, and then Lydia commented on Thomas' dress shirt and tie. Then she asked him if he had left her for another woman. Thomas tried to explain to her that it was the circumstances and not the woman, but Lydia would hear nothing of it. She let him know that when he had called that night, everything was packed and ready to go. She was leaving her position at the hospital, her friends, her family, and her life—all for him. What had he done for her? How about total humiliation for starters. Lydia remained composed as she told him that the year was very difficult for her because of the questions that were left unanswered. She thought that they had created a solid bond between them and couldn't believe or accept that she could have been so completely wrong about him and about them.

As Thomas sat listening to her, he realized that she was right. Everything that she said was indisputable. He had walked away without looking back, as if there had never been anything or anyone there to walk away from. Lydia had made him realize that living together was more than playing house and being intimate. Really living together was a commitment and not a game. Even when Thomas had asked Ann if they could live together, it was to save money on rent. He was attracted to her, but that was just another reason to live together. Maybe Ann had sensed that from him. Maybe that was the reason that she wasn't coming back. Thomas was confused. Did he have to commit to marriage as part of the deal for either of them?

Thomas then asked Lydia if she had thought about them getting married at some point when they were together? Lydia was amazed at Thomas' naiveté. What did he think? Was every relationship a dress rehearsal for another relationship? They parted company for the evening, and Thomas said that he would call her tomorrow. Lydia said good night.

The next day, Thomas spoke with Ann. She told him that the company had refused to change the terms of her contract, and she wasn't returning. The apartment was no problem because she was not on a lease. Thomas remembered that he was not on a lease either. He thought to himself that maybe he should return to Boston, but he really liked his job; he loved it. Ann asked him to please come out to California and spend some time with her. She did not sound very corporate anymore like she did at the board meetings.

Thomas visited with his family for the next few days. He spent some time working in the antique shop and re-establishing ties with friends and relatives. He called Lydia a few times, but she was working double shifts and was unable to see him. When he finally did speak with her, she said that she needed more time to think about things before seeing him again.

Thomas relaxed during his final night in Boston. He knew that it was going to be difficult to catch up with all the work that needed to be done. After all, Ann was no longer part of the equation, and most likely he would be asked to fill in for her until someone new was hired.

"No Heartache"

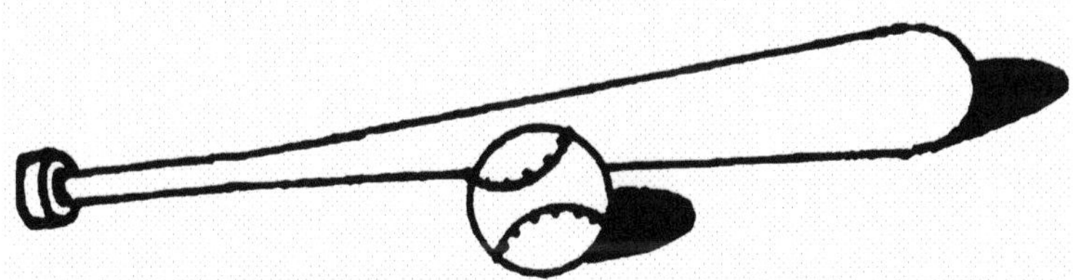

Len Lyons was not as healthy as the rest of the ten year olds on the baseball team. In those days, he had what was called—a "heart condition." Today, his medical problem would most likely be described as a congenital heart defect. What Len did not have was the energy or robust coloring of a healthy person, but what he did have was the determination or "heart of a lion" which is why his last name was so appropriate.

Len's team was made up of Little League 'B' division players who would eventually graduate to the 'A' division if things worked out for them on the field or from behind the scenes. Len just wanted to play, but he found it difficult to participate because he became winded very quickly. There were many times when Len did not even practice with the team or make it to the games.

Most of his teammates were not big on showing very much compassion, and Len wasn't looking for it. All he desired was to be seen as a regular kid who just wanted to win like everyone else. The coaches of the team were a married couple who seemed to have a tremendous amount of empathy for children as well as a pretty good knowledge of baseball. They encouraged their players to do their best and not worry too much about the score, but winning was the object of the game.

On a dusty hot day at the Point Shirley baseball field, Len made it to the starting line-up. Most of his teammates were surprised, and some were annoyed, but the coaches reminded them that they were a team. With the score tied near the end of the game, it was Len's turn to bat, and he walked up to the plate. On the very first pitch, he hit the ball as far as or farther than anyone had done all year. His teammates began to yell and scream wildly as Len ran to first base.

The coaches settled everyone down and looked towards the on deck hitter; what happened next was totally unexpected. Len's team was well aware of his medical problem and that Len would most likely be out of breath after his run to first base, but apparently Len was not going to let his 'condition' slow him down—no way. He knew from the distance of his mighty hit that it absolutely should be a home run, and he was going for it. Len rounded second base and suddenly began to lose speed. As Len approached third base, he was barely running, and the opposing team now had the ball. They were throwing it towards the infield.

Len's teammates pleaded with him to stop at third base. They were more than satisfied with a triple, but Len wasn't going for any triple. He started towards home plate, and about half way there, he just collapsed. At this point, nobody was thinking about Len's hit anymore because he was now crawling. As he got closer and closer to within a few feet of his final destination, the catcher caught the relay throw and then tagged him out.

Len slowly made it back up to his feet and walked over to the bench with help from the coaches. He sat down, still gasping for air. As his teammates ridiculed him for trying to score, Len looked up; he was totally exhausted. Some of his teammates continued yelling at him while others were laughing at his fool-hearty attempt to keep going around the base path. Len raised his head up from his knees and wiped the sweat from the back of his neck. His teammates continued to vent their frustration in his direction, and Len looked up again, still laboring in his breathing. He'd take all the ridicule and criticism over anyone's pity. Unexpectedly and without any prompting from the coaches, a few of the players walked over to him, patted him on the back and then said, "Nice hit."

Len nodded.

"Markers"

David B. Tick

Lisa, Joel, & Jerry

My first real encounter with death was at the ripe old age of six or seven; I'm not quite sure. I just remember that it was the worst experience of my life up to that point. Lisa was in my first grade class at the Shirley Street School, and forty-five years later, I still see her parents around the town where I've lived for most of my life. (Sometimes I feel like Jimmy Stewart in *It's a Wonderful Life*.) I never say "hello" if I see them. I mean, I'd like to identify myself because they've known my family for years. But what good would it do? It would just remind them of what had happened to their precious child, and that's why I have no relationship with them. There's a very good chance that I wouldn't have one anyway, but... I'll probably never know.

Lisa had leukemia for over a year and even though I prayed for her almost every night, she died. It was such a helpless feeling for all of us who knew her. I think that's when I first learned the word... *agnostic*. Lisa was a really quiet girl in school, and I don't remember if we spoke much... or even at all; but when I think about one of my very first heroes, she would be at the top of the list.

My first grade teacher never smiled or made us feel comfortable. Twenty-five years later, I saw her while she was volunteering at the local hospital. I never realized that she was such a tiny woman but to a first grader, she seemed like a monster. One day, she whacked me on the head with a ruler, and I cried in front of the class. The reason *why* she hit me was rather comical: Somebody in the back of the room had actually crapped on the floor. That feat alone was more amazing to us than disgusting, so we turned it into an adventure! Very slowly, the crap started to make its way toward the front of the room, and this was done in a fine cooperative spirit, courtesy of the students in our row. (We used our pencils.) Unfortunately for me, I was one of the last students to move the load. Suddenly I looked up, and there she was with ruler in hand. *Smack*! I told my parents about it, and I think they spoke with her because she never hit anyone again.

Elementary school was a very complicated time for my little mind; ironically, the movie *West Side Story* helped to reinforce that confusion by creating schisms among various ethnic and socio-economic groups. Imagine ten-year-old suburban kids running around, trying to act like "Sharks" and "Jets." Very few really fought like the gangs in the inner cities, but it helped to create differences that we had never really noticed too much before. The older kids had "rumbles" with neighboring towns and cities. I don't think that their gang fights could be attributed to the musical. For us, those divisions would continue right through high school.

It seems that art in just about any form can affect the masses; it's just difficult to predict exactly what that impact might be. Imagine, Leonard Bernstein was trying to make us aware of prejudice and stereotypes; but instead, we modeled those negative attitudes and perceptions.

Behind my house was a huge lot that we called *The Field*. That's where we all played baseball, army, attack of the aliens, tag, and everything else. There were so many rocks and pieces of glass in that dirt pit, we never learned how to catch a "true bounce." Any time I tried to keep my head down and my eyes on the ball like you're supposed to... *smash*... right in the face! I never even realized until much later on in life when I was on a softball team, that you could predict the bounce of a ball and might actually be able to field it without getting ready to pull back your head to survive what was coming.

We all loved the field, though. There was no grass except for weeds with prickly stickers, and thousands of grasshoppers. The jungle portion of the field was located behind and around the summer cottage about twenty yards from my house. There were these tall, cool looking plants. I think it was rhubarb, but to us it was definitely... bamboo!

At the top of the field was a large house with oversized windows. We would "borrow" my father's golf clubs and hit golf balls "over" the house, trying to reach the beach. Unfortunately, we broke most of the windows in the process. Some of those drives just went too low. The owner of the house was constantly repairing them. He eventually boarded up most of the windows and re-shingled one half of the entire house. I couldn't understand why he had such an "attitude" against us. I guess he didn't like golf.

One time my brother and I were in the field, throwing a fiberglass boomerang that *really worked*. On about the third toss, it magnificently floated away in the distance... but upon its sweeping return, two more windows—GONE. This time it was the second floor porch of the adjacent house to ours. We couldn't believe it because the boomerang broke through one window and almost came out through the other one. Being so excited about its amazing return flight, we temporarily forgot that we had to ring our neighbor's bell in order to retrieve it. I think they would have figured it out, even if we hadn't confessed. There weren't too many kids with boomerangs in the area. We had to pay for those windows, but I don't think *we* actually paid. That was a parental responsibility.

At the top of the field in another yard near the house with the windows, we used to play whiffleball, mostly at night. There was this "older" guy named Joel who lived on the next street. He was an *Eagle Scout,* but he wasn't very "clean and reverent" towards us, so we didn't like him at all. He constantly harassed us, and we would swear at him. One day, he suddenly died from spinal meningitis at the age of thirteen. As children, our feelings were so conflicted. I wish that we had been friends instead of enemies. His family was shattered and never did recover from the tragedy. He must have been a good kid. How else do you become an "Eagle Scout?"

Within a year of Joel's death, my brother's best friend also died from an illness at the age of thirteen. Jerry had a congenital immunodeficiency disease. When he passed away, the loss was devastating for my brother. They had grown up together and were inseparable. It was a sad time for all of us. Jerry was another one of my early heroes.

In elementary school, my fifth grade teacher was definitely my favorite; he had an engaging personality and made us feel good about ourselves… but for the students who didn't work in class, they were kept back at the end of the year. One of the effects of the "baby-boom" was a need for more space; consequently, our classroom was situated in the auditorium. Being away from the rest of the school made us feel special. Sometimes we would go to the stage area, and the teacher would ask me to play a song on the grand piano for the class. I was *really* shy, but he seemed to have so much confidence in me… it was easy to do.

During those early school years, we used to have air raid sirens to "prepare" us for a sudden nuclear attack. We were too young to know what was really going on, but the idea of hiding under your desk to avoid the effects of a nuclear blast seemed a little ridiculous. There were just too many pictures of the atomic bomb being dropped on Hiroshima. On the other hand, the bomb shelter in the school's basement… now that made sense!

Nana (Nanny) and Grandma

I had a completely different relationship with my mother's mother (Nana/Nanny) from the one I had with my father's mother (Grandma). I was named for my grandfather, who passed away a few days after I was born. My Nana lived two streets over from us in an apartment building where my family lived, before buying our house. She had high blood pressure and they didn't have medications to treat it back then, so she suffered from strokes. When I was nine, she died of heart failure. The family took it very hard. I remember that Nana was always smiling. Even when she wasn't feeling that well, she was so happy to see her grandchildren when we might drop by unexpectedly; that was just her nature.

Nana was married to "Pop." I thought he was my grandfather until one day while driving in the car, my mother and brother informed me that "Pop" was actually my step-grandfather. Pop was an odd guy, who did some weird things, but he also had a great sense of humor. All of the kids on the street really liked him. Pop was beyond eccentric… something more like obsessive-compulsive. For example, he would always wash his hands after touching a doorknob or our dog, Taffy, pop's best friend after Nana passed away. One vivid memory that I have of him is that he used to break up fights between my brother and me when my parents went out for the night. Usually it would be on Saturday and my brother was stuck watching me. We'd end up throwing things at each other, breaking an antique or two, and maybe a window. Ironically, after Pop would stop the fight, my brother and I would become fast friends as we desperately tried to glue the broken objects together. It would be months until the items were discovered in their "repaired" condition. Fortunately for us, the delayed time factor of discovery always played to our advantage.

Pop didn't look it but physically he was "in shape" despite having diabetes, and the man was a character. He could down a half-gallon of coffee ice cream in about twenty minutes.

Pop died about fourteen years after Nana. He was a really good grandfather, even with his odd behaviors.

My connection with Grandma was not that strong. She favored my aunt's children, probably because she lived with them for a long time. Eventually she moved right down the street from us and remarried. Sadly, she and her new husband both passed away a couple of years later, but I was glad that we had some time to get a little closer.

During those years in "The Fifties," my older sister used to have rock and roll "sock hops" in our basement, which was fixed up pretty nicely. I used to pretend that I was a dog, walking on all fours and barking. Okay, I was strange... but it did give me the opportunity to sneak up on them when the music stopped and they were "necking."

Uncle Arthur and Terry

Uncle Arthur wasn't my real uncle, but he was closer than any "real" uncle that I had. Tougher than tough, he had marched with Patton and didn't back down from anyone or anything. He lived upstairs from my family for many years and was one of my father's closest friends. In 1962, Arthur was diagnosed with lung cancer and had a lung removed. For two years, I prayed for him and thought he was going to get better, but in the spring of 1964, he died. My favorite "Arthur" memory is when he would come home from work in his blue Thunderbird *hardtop* convertible. In the good weather, it was a daily ritual for his family and our family to watch this fantastic top, as it went up and down with its metal sections that actually folded into the trunk.

Just before Arthur died, Terry died from Hodgkin's disease. Terry was in her early thirties and lived across the street from us with five children. She and my mother were good friends right up until the day Terry died. It was a very rough time. I remember going to her son's birthday party, and you'd never know anything was wrong with her. A few months after the party, I was late (my only time) for junior high school, and a friend of the family saw me walking and gave me a ride. She told me that Terry had died that morning, so I actually knew about it before her son, who sat next to me. I remember seeing him in school when I got to class, and the emotional pain that I felt for him was overwhelming, but I didn't say a word; a few minutes later he was called to the office. Because I was *tardy* that day, I was given detention. The idea of punishment for being late after what had just happened seemed absurd to me... I mean *death* had visited the school... my friend had lost his mother! Didn't anybody get it? I certainly wasn't articulate enough to express that or anything else for that matter, so I stayed the hour, sitting in the mandatory silence... helpless. My high school experience was definitely better, but the prevailing authoritarian style of teaching always left me feeling uncomfortable and rebellious. Things changed in college, when I finally began to enjoy the educational process.

Joyce and Uncle Ben

After graduating from U-Mass with a degree in English in 1973, I played keyboard and wrote songs for a band called "Some of My Best Friends." I lived in a large house with some of the members of the group in Sunderland, Massachusetts, which is about seven miles north of Amherst. It was an interesting time in that we were able to totally sustain ourselves at the ages of twenty-one to twenty-four as musicians, without working other jobs. I could have been a better keyboard player if I had been focused more on the technical and theoretical aspects of music, and less on the "lifestyle" of being a musician.

One night at the band house, I received a phone call from my parents. My friend Joyce had died, suddenly. She was like family. Every summer, she had come to the beach for two months with her parents and sisters, and lived in that cottage behind our house *surrounded by the jungle in the field*. She and my brother had dated for about a year, before he went abroad. I was also told that my Uncle Ben had died. Both funerals were to be held in the same temple… one right after the other. The next day, I drove to my hometown to get ready. The funeral for Joyce was a nightmare. I don't know for sure how she died, but I think she may have had an eating disorder. When I walked into the chapel, everybody was crying including me. I hugged her two sisters as tight as I could. We were all in shock. She was only in her mid-twenties! After everyone *except my family* left for the burial grounds, I watched the funeral director change the placard and put up my Uncle's name.

After the chapel service for Uncle Ben, my cousin (his son) conducted an Orthodox Jewish service at their house because they were very religious. When it was over, he asked me when I had found out. As I was answering him, I realized that I was talking about when I had heard about Joyce. I was in a daze. I still think about her when I drive down Commonwealth Avenue in Boston, which is near where her family lived. I never see my cousin.

"The Baby" and Gerry

In 1976, I moved back home after seven years (four years of college and three years on the road). The band had broken up, and I was unemployed. All I wanted to do was get another band going. I had no plans to do anything else but continue to be a musician. The problem was that I could not recreate what I had in Amherst. I also was experiencing somewhat of a "culture shock." For seven years I had lived away from the Boston area, and I had become more country than city. Upon moving home, I fell into a depression. I tried for two years to form another band, but it just didn't work out; the dream was slipping away. Working part-time for a marketing research company at minimum wage was my primary source of income, although I did work with a band for a few months. I was lost and regressing intellectually, emotionally, and creatively.

Another reason why the music scene began to fade for me was that I was an original music kind of guy, and "Disco" was sweeping the nation. Looking back, I think it was a post-war celebration after Vietnam. Musicians were only hired if they played that kind of music. It was really a D.J. gig, now. Still, I moved to Providence, Rhode Island and joined a Disco band. We never worked, but we ate well and had some fun. I made a few dollars working construction for a couple of weeks.

One late afternoon in Providence, I received a phone call from my mother who was crying on the other end. She told me that "the baby" had died. At first, I thought she was talking about my younger sister. Then she mentioned Paris where my brother and his French wife lived. It was their baby... delivered stillborn. I was stunned! The baby would have been the first grandchild and my nephew. I felt so powerless, especially since my brother lived in Europe. I wish that I could have helped him, but I was incapable of helping anybody... including myself.

Within a couple weeks, I left Providence and returned home again. My father and I went to a Christmas party, and I met the brother of his law partner. He was president of a property insurance company and offered me a job.

With a terrible economy and having zero money, I accepted, gratefully… just in time for the "Blizzard of 78."

It was about a year later when my next-door neighbor, Gerry, became ill and died from cancer. He was my older sister's age and our families were very friendly. Gerry always took the time to ask how things were going. He was a great guy with a great smile... always genuine!

The idea of a 9-5 job with one week's vacation the first year seemed fine to me after struggling for two years trying to get a new band together. I eventually worked my way up to the position of "claims examiner." As I began to make more money, think I was actually important, and date some of the women in the office who were as immature as I was, things were changing. At a party, an older guy from one of the firms I hired to do property inspections gave me a ride home one night and told me the score. Basically, I was a jerk who had a little power now. I took it to heart… it was just that I was not in control of who I was anymore. I had lost my identity.

During that time in my life, I studied Kung Fu for a few months. This came about after an incident that occurred on Revere Beach. I had gone to the movies with a friend of mine, and later that night we stopped at *Billy's Dry Dock* to meet some friends. After leaving a short time later because it was late, we were walking towards my car when all of a sudden from across the street I heard someone yell, "Hey you…you're dead!"

I answered him, "Who? Me?"

He yelled back, "Yeah! You!"

I proceeded to squeeze my arm for a few seconds and then say, "No I'm not." I guess I was a comedian that night.

He didn't think that my response was too funny, so he informed me that I was going to have to fight him because I was with his girlfriend (definitely not my type). I told him that I wasn't with her; she was just a friend, but that didn't stop him. He was drunk and wasn't really a threat. In the middle of the boulevard, he attacked me. It wasn't much of a fight. I even went to *Kelly's* right after to get some clam chowder.

Now I was never a tough guy; I hate violence and just wasn't brought up that way. Basically I responded emotionally and rationally to someone's irrational challenge. That can be a problem when dealing with people who choose to use violence to express themselves and don't have the intelligence or emotional capacity to work things out.

The next day, one of my coworkers from the insurance company saw me with a few bruises on my face and asked me what had happened. I told her the story, and she introduced me to her boyfriend who was a kung fu instructor. I studied with him, privately, and picked up a few moves; but the most important thing that I learned from him was to react without thinking. Thinking was dangerous when dealing with people who *didn't* think.

During the afternoon of the Celtic's 1981 championship celebration, I was partying outside with a huge crowd of fans at City Hall Plaza. It was at that moment that I realized I could no longer be in the insurance business. In some ways I liked being a claims examiner; it had its challenges, but it just wasn't right for me.

I took the summer off and six months later after working as an appliance salesman, I left for the western part of the state. I was going to start another band. In early

January, I packed up the car and left. Maybe it wasn't a realistic goal, but one thing was for sure; I needed to get back to the country!

Jackie and "The Captain"

Before returning to the Amherst/Northampton area in 1982, I received word that the singer of our band from my post-college years had died of complications from lupus. Jackie was a very tall, African-American woman who went to Smith College, the same school that my older sister had attended ten years earlier. Jackie *made* our band with her dynamic style and soulful voice. When she left the group, we couldn't sustain it without her, despite our strong original material. She was awesome, and then we became ordinary. I remember that during our years together in the group after college, Jackie suffered from a chronic sore throat, which was attributed to vocal stress. Actually, it was probably an early sign of the lupus. She ultimately became a successful lawyer in Louisville, Kentucky and was doing really well. Then suddenly she was gone, but her voice and her spirit will always be with me.

Moving back to the area after five years away was a nice change. I rented out a room from an old college friend who had once lived at the band house. Putting together a new group was not that difficult because there were some very good musicians in the area, but we didn't work too much. Money got really tight after about six months. The Pioneer Valley was very, very hot that June, so I wanted to get out of there. The Valley's charm had disappeared for me, but I wasn't ready to go back to the Boston area. I saw an advertisement to work at a camp in New Hampshire, so I took the job. I lasted three weeks.

About a month later, I was an appliance salesman again... but things were going to be different! After working at the camp with inner-city kids, it made me realize that I might like to teach.

When I settled back at home, I heard that "The Captain" had been killed in Florida. Captain Vornado was actually named for the brand of air conditioning unit on his stepfather's cab. Our mutual friend, and resident guru, as a joke, gave the name to him. The name stuck. Captain and I were in a few bands together, and he was a very good drummer. I remember one time when we were hanging out at the beach; he pulled out a gun and started shooting rapid fire into the water... I avoided him after that. He had potential but chose the wrong path in life, and it caught up with him.

Eventually, I returned to school for my teaching certification, and then to graduate school. Unfortunately, there were very few teaching jobs available. In fact, budget cuts were forcing teacher layoffs.

Since that time, more than twenty years have passed, and so many more have left us. There's an emptiness that follows… the void can never be filled. Recently, at my classmate's funeral, a friend shared some inspirational words that I think would make an appropriate conclusion: "If we could just give each other love, all of our lives would be so much richer for ***whatever time*** we have." Sometimes it's the struggles that inspire us to reflect upon who we were… and who ***they*** were.

When we look to the future
the present is lost
in a dream of tomorrow…

So hold on to the minutes
because there are clouds of change…

By listening to the seconds ticking,
the reflection of your being emerges today
in a universe of light speed…

As you inhale and exhale,
let the quietness of your mind speak to you…

Listen…

Critical Thinking and Writing

"New England Home Grown"

1. Who is your favorite character and why?

2. What impact does their <u>bond of friendship</u> have upon the boys' lives?

3. If Jimbo is one of the protagonists in the story, explain how Rocco and Jimbo's father might be considered antagonists.

"Brian"

1. What happened to Brian?

2. Why didn't the *three* of them ever meet up again after college?

3. What is the author's tone throughout the story? Why?

4. What does "the idealism of Woodstock was supplanted by the hedonistic days of Disco" mean?

5. How does the ending reflect a central theme that is repeated during the story?

"The Taste of Medicine"

1. Contrast the personalities of Cameron and Peggy.

2. Would you consider Peggy's *dishonesty* justifiable? Why/Why Not?

3. Discuss how power and revenge are important to the theme: Give specific examples from the plot.

"Ant Lessons"

1. Compare/contrast "book knowledge" and "real life experience" in the story.

2. How did the philosophy book contribute to the author's personal growth?

3. What inner changes did the author experience and when?

4. Describe a situation in which you wanted to achieve a certain goal; however, you were not quite emotionally, psychologically, or intellectually ready at that stage in your life.

"A Night Out"

1. Who was Danny? What did he do for a living?

2. What foreshadowing events made Danny suspicious of Tom Porter?

3. In what way did Danny ignore his "gut feeling" about meeting with Tom?

4. How does irony play a role in the ending of the story? Be specific!

"The End of Superman"

1. Give an example of a personal experience from your childhood that parallels this story.

2. How is *Superman* a metaphor for innocence?

3. In what two ways did an unnecessary "passing comment" change the little boy?

4. Describe how teasing is sometimes damaging to a child's self-image.

"For Better or For Worse"

1. How does the setting contribute to the development of the theme?

2. What is your opinion of bachelor parties? Explain...

3. In what way does the title of the story relate to the plot?

"A Simple Solution"

1. What does this story imply about good intentions?

2. How did stress affect the decision making capability of the main character?

3. Why are "simple solutions" not always the best solutions?

"Pencil Me In"

1. Describe the main characters in the story.

2. In what way is the title of the story directly related to the theme?

3. Choose a character from the story with whom you identify. Why?

"No Heartache"

1. After his hit, why didn't Len stop at first base?

2. Did Len's teammates have the right to react in the way that they did? Why/Why Not?

3. From the points of view of the coaches, Len, and the team – examine some of the *inner conflicts* that may have existed while Len was going for the home run.

"Markers"

1. How does the author use "stream-of-consciousness" as a writing technique?

2. In what two ways does the title of the story relate to the events that occur?

3. Describe the "markers" in *your* life and what impact they have had upon you.

About the Author

David B. Tick is a writing instructor in the Boston area. He also specializes in curriculum development and alternative teaching styles. His e-mail address is www.communitylearningpress.com.

www.ingramcontent.com/pod-product-compliance
Ingram Content Group UK Ltd.
Pitfield, Milton Keynes, MK11 3LW, UK
UKHW040016200726
13854UKWH00001B/227

9 780759 662827